BLACK CROW, BLACK CROW

by Ginger Foglesong Guy
pictures by
Nancy Winslow Parker

GREENWILLOW BOOKS, NEW YORK

Watercolor paints, colored pencils, and a black pen were used for the
full-color art. The text type is ITC New Baskerville Semibold.
Text copyright © 1991 by Ginger Foglesong Guy
Illustrations copyright © 1991 by Nancy Winslow Parker
Greenwillow Books, a division of William Morrow & Company, Inc.,
105 Madison Avenue, New York, NY 10016.   Printed in Hong Kong by
South China Printing Company (1988) Ltd.   First Edition   10 9 8 7 6 5 4 3 2 1

Library of Congress Cataloging-in-Publication Data
Guy, Ginger Foglesong.
Black crow, black crow / by Ginger Foglesong Guy ;
pictures by Nancy Winslow Parker.
p.   cm.
Summary: High up in a tree, a mother crow tends her young.
ISBN 0-688-08956-9.   ISBN 0-688-08957-7 (lib. bdg.)
[1. Crows—Fiction.   2. Mother and child—Fiction.]
I. Parker, Nancy Winslow, ill.   II. Title.
PZ7.G9865B1   1991
[E]—dc20   89-34619   CIP   AC

FOR
ANDY
G.F.G.

FOR
PETER GAUNTT
N.W.P.

Black crow , black crow,
what do you caw about?

What do you jaw about
high in your tree?

I wake up my children,
my small sleeping children.

I wake up my children
high up in my tree.

Black crow , black crow ,
what do you caw about?

What do you jaw about
high in the leaves?

I feed all my children,
my hungry young children.

I feed all my children
high up in the leaves.

Black crow , black crow ,
what do you caw about?

What do you jaw about
high in the sky?

I play with my children,
my lively young children.

I play with my children,
high up in the sky.

Black crow , black crow,
what do you caw about?

What do you jaw about
high on the wire?

I call to my children,
my tired young children.

I call to my children
high up on the wire.

Black crow  , black crow ,
what do you caw about?

What do you jaw about
at home in your nest?

I sing to my children,
my small sleepy children.

I sing to my children
at home in our nest.

Shhhhh....

JP   GUY
        BLACK CROW, BLACK CROW
GUY